Chicken Man

The Library of Congress has cataloged the Lothrop, Lee & Shepard Books
edition of Chicken Man *as follows:*
Edwards, Michelle. Chicken man/by Michelle Edwards.
p. cm. Summary: Each time Chicken Man is moved into a new job on the kibbutz,
someone else wants to take that job instead, and the chickens suffer as a consequence.
ISBN 0-688-09708-1.—ISBN 0-688-09709-X (lib. bdg.) [1. Kibbutzim—Fiction.
2. Occupations—Fiction. 3. Chickens—Fiction. 4. Israel—Fiction.
5. Jews—Israel—Fiction.] I. Title.
PZ7.E262Ch 1991 [E]—dc20 90-32625 CIP AC

3 5 7 9 10 8 6 4 2
First Mulberry Edition, 1994
ISBN 0-688-13106-9

to Ricardo and Isabel

Kibbutz Hanan

Chicken Man

Michelle Edwards

A Mulberry Paperback Book

New York

Deep in Israel's Jezreel Valley there once lived a man known to his mother as Rody and to all the rest of Kibbutz Hanan as Chicken Man.

Now, you might wonder why Rody would choose a name like Chicken Man. He didn't. But the summer he worked in the kibbutz chicken coop, the hens laid more eggs than ever before and the roosters strutted and crowed as if they were the happiest in all of Israel. That's when the kibbutz started calling Rody Chicken Man.

Chicken Man liked the chicken coop. He liked chickens. He liked all the noisy clucking when he sang. He even liked the way Clara greeted him by landing on his head and hugging his kibbutz hat.

Chicken Man thought that he might like to work in the chicken coop forever. But in those days, everyone on a kibbutz had to take a turn at all the jobs. Some jobs were outside in the fields and orchards. Most everyone liked those jobs. Other jobs no one wanted to do, like baking cookies all day long in the big, hot kibbutz oven. That was Bracha's job when Rody became Chicken Man, and she hated it. What's more, no one liked her cookies.

Bracha went to see Simon, the head of the work committee.

"I want Chicken Man's job," she told him. "The chickens are always so happy, and they are so easy to please."

So when the new work list was posted, Bracha moved to the chicken coop and Chicken Man was sent to the laundry.

It wasn't easy for Chicken Man to trade his chickens for a washing machine and an iron, but he did.

"Good-bye, my dears. I'll visit often," he promised. And with one last pat for Clara, Chicken Man set off for the laundry.

On his first morning, surrounded by bags and bags of dirty clothes, Chicken Man began to sing—old songs, new songs, folk songs, songs of the pioneers.

Every day, Chicken Man sang while he worked. The laundry was a quiet place, no clucking or crowing anywhere. But when Chicken Man sang, the noise of the chicken coop didn't seem so far away. The louder Chicken Man sang, the closer his chickens seemed.

Chicken Man sang so loudly that Dov could hear him in the dairy. As Dov milked the cows and mucked out the barn, he thought about how much he would like a job in a clean place like the laundry, where he could sing as loud as he liked without being kicked by a cow.

Dov went to talk to Simon. When the new work list was posted, Dov moved to the laundry. And Chicken Man?

"Meet the new kibbutz gardener," Chicken Man told the chickens. The roosters crowed sadly and the hens sat quietly. They missed Chicken Man and he missed them.

Clara pecked at her feathers. "I'll bring you flowers from the garden," he promised her.

In Chicken Man's first week as gardener, he weeded and mulched and trimmed. He even fixed the sprinkler system. And every night he brought Clara a bunch of bright red roses.

Every morning, from her window in the kitchen, Aviva watched Chicken Man watering the roses. While she washed the big pots and pans in steaming hot water, she could see Chicken Man climbing the big old lemon tree to trim the dead branches. Ah—to be high in a shady lemon tree! To cover roses with a cool, steady stream of water! No wonder Chicken Man was always singing!

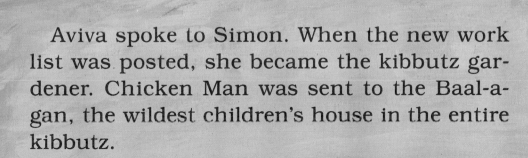

Aviva spoke to Simon. When the new work list was posted, she became the kibbutz gardener. Chicken Man was sent to the Baal-a-gan, the wildest children's house in the entire kibbutz.

The roosters shook their sagging combs and the hens pecked and poked at his boots when Chicken Man told them about his new job. They weren't the same happy brood. He was worried about them.

"I'll be back tomorrow," he promised.

The next morning Chicken Man walked to the Baal-a-gan to cook breakfast. The children were wilder than ever. Gabi was dumping oatmeal in Eli's bed. Eli, Hannah, and Matan were making their chairs and tables into a wobbly tower. Mira and Shira were unrolling a roll of toilet paper to see whether it would really stretch to Tel Aviv.

"Hey, look at this," said Chicken Man, juggling spoons.

"Pancakes, anyone?" he asked as he tossed a few eggs in the air.

That morning the children didn't throw a single pancake. They ate their breakfast and laughed while Chicken Man juggled oranges.

Just then Moshe passed by on his way to work in the orchard. He looked into the Baal-a-gan and laughed. Apple trees were pretty, but trimming and pruning weren't much fun. He was just thinking about how much he would like to work in the Baal-a-gan, when in ran Simon, huffing and puffing.

There was trouble in the chicken coop. The hens had stopped laying eggs!

"No eggs for cakes!" shouted Simon. "No eggs for cookies! No eggs for the kibbutz to sell!"

"Oy va voy!" said Chicken Man. He should have known it would come to this. Poor Clara! "Get the work committee together!"

Simon called a meeting for that afternoon.

"The chickens need me," Chicken Man told the committee.

"And the kibbutz needs eggs," added Simon. "Chicken Man is the only one who can make our hens happy again. We need him back in the chicken coop."

The work committee agreed. No more job switching for Chicken Man. He could work in the chicken coop now and forever.

Chicken Man hurried out of the meeting and went straight to the chicken coop.

"Cock-a-doodle-do!" he sang to the roosters.

"I'm back!" he sang to the hens.

Chicken Man sang a few of their favorite songs. The chickens began to cluck and crow. Clara flew to her special spot on top of his head. And the next morning, every hen laid an extra egg.

Chicken Man was home.

A Note from the Author

In Israel, there are special farms called kibbutzim. Kibbutzniks (the people who live and work on those farms) work as hard and as much as they can, and the kibbutz gives them food, clothing, and a place to live in return. The kibbutzniks live in different little houses, but they all eat together in the big kibbutz dining hall.

All kinds of fruit and vegetables are grown on a kibbutz. Cotton and wheat are also grown, and animals are raised as well. Most kibbutzim make things, too, such as toys or funiture. One kibbutz, Kibbutz Ein Gedi, makes animated movies for the Israeli "Sesame Street" show, *Rehov SumSum.*

Kibbutz Hanan is a made-up kibbutz in a real place, the Jezreel valley. The first kibbutzim were just like Kibbutz Hanan: the kibbutzniks moved about from job to job, and the children lived in special little houses with other children their age. Today if you visit Israel, you will see that each kibbutz is different. But who knows? When you visit, you still might meet someone like Chicken Man. I did.